Lula
and the
SEA MONSTER

Alex Latimer

PEACHTREE
ATLANTA

Published by
PEACHTREE PUBLISHING COMPANY INC.
1700 Chattahoochee Avenue
Atlanta, Georgia 30318-2112
www.peachtree-online.com

Text and illustrations © 2018 by Alex Latimer

First published in Great Britain in 2018 by Oxford University Press
First United States edition published in 2019 by Peachtree Publishing Company Inc.

The illustrations were created as pencil drawings, digitized, then finished with color and texture.

Printed in 2019 in China
10 9 8 7 6 5 4 3 2 1
First Edition

ISBN: 978-1-68263-122-5

Library of Congress Cataloging-in-Publication Data
Names: Latimer, Alex, author, illustrator.
Title: Lula and the sea monster / written and illustrated by Alex Latimer.
Description: First edition. | Atlanta : Peachtree Publishing Company Inc., 2019. | Summary: Lula and her parents must leave their
beloved house on the beach, but Bean, the tiny creature she rescued from a seagull, becomes a friend and does not want her to go.
Identifiers: LCCN 2018044608 | ISBN 9781682631225
Subjects: | CYAC: Sea monsters—Fiction. | Friendship—Fiction. | Beaches—Fiction. | Moving, Household—Fiction.
Classification: LCC PZ7.L369612 Lul 2019 | DDC [E]—dc23
LC record available at *https://lccn.loc.gov/2018044608*

Lula lived in an old house on the beach with her parents. She loved looking for things that washed up on the sand and watching the animals that lived in the rock pools.

But none of that would last much longer. In a few days, Lula and her family would have to move.

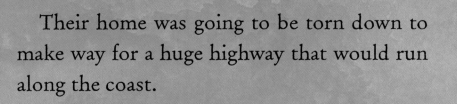

Their home was going to be torn down to
make way for a huge highway that would run
along the coast.

Early one morning, Lula packed some sandwiches and took her bucket and spade.

She went for a walk along the beach, combing for treasures while she still could.

Further down the shore, she noticed a seagull
snapping at something in a small rock pool.

Lula chased the seagull away.

Then she scooped up the tiniest creature in her bucket.

He curled around Lula's finger, happy to have been rescued.

"Look how little you are," said Lula. "You're hardly bigger than a bean. Oh! That's what I'll call you—Bean!"

Bean seemed much too small to look after himself in the deep, wide ocean. So Lula put him in a larger rock pool with plenty of crevices to hide from hungry seagulls.

She gave Bean a sandwich from her backpack, and Bean gobbled it up. Lula spent the whole day with her new friend.

"It's getting late," Lula told Bean, "but I'll be back tomorrow." Then she headed for home.

Lula woke up early the next morning, made three extra sandwiches, and hurried along the beach to see her new friend. But the tiny creature she had left in the rock pool...

...had grown overnight!
Now Bean was too big for the pool.
Lula would have to find him a new home.

So she scooped Bean up in her bucket, though he hardly fit,

and dragged the bucket to a larger pool.

Lula gave Bean all of the sandwiches she'd brought—even her own. Lula stayed as long as she could, and they played until sunset. It was getting harder to say good-bye.

The next day, Lula packed all the food she could carry, stuffed it in a bed sheet,

and dragged it to Bean's pool.

Bean had grown even bigger!
There was no way Lula
could carry him now.

So Lula lured Bean to an extra-large rock pool with the food she'd brought.

They spent hours of fun together, and it was the greatest day two friends could have.

When it was time to go home, Lula felt terribly sad. Soon she would have to move away and leave Bean forever.

The next morning, Lula felt miserable as she packed her things.
She was already missing Bean a great deal.

So Lula put some pickles, potatoes, and crackers in a box and set off to see Bean one last time.

But Bean wasn't in his pool. She couldn't find him anywhere.

Lula sat beside the empty rock pool for ages, but she never got the chance to say good-bye.

On moving day, Lula watched her mum and dad pack the last of their belongings into their car. They looked as sad as she felt. Then came the roar of bulldozers.

"Lula," her parents called, "it's time for us to go."

But Lula wouldn't go. She couldn't. This was their home!
And not just her family's! This stretch of beach was home to
millions of creatures—creatures like her friend, Bean.

So Lula marched over to the bulldozers.

"I'm not going anywhere!" she shouted.

The men laughed.

"I mean it!" Lula yelled.

But the bulldozers crept forward, puffing black smoke into the air.

It was no use.
Lula turned to get one last look at her house...

And there was Bean—
bigger than ten elephants!

He curled around Lula's
home the way he'd curled
around her finger the first
day they met.

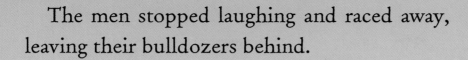

The men stopped laughing and raced away,
leaving their bulldozers behind.

Lula still lives in her house with her parents.
And there is no highway on the beach.

Of course the bulldozers
came back, three more times
actually,

but each time Bean
chased them away.

Lula still walks along the sand every day, searching for interesting things and animals that need looking after. And most days, Bean swims along in the shallows.

They couldn't be happier.